Hannah's Alaska

Story by
Joanne Reiser

Illustrations by
Julie Downing

A Carnival Press Book　　Raintree Publishers Inc.

To Howard and all our sons and daughters:
Gwenn, Kurt, Lisa, Andrea, Gregory,
Christopher and Annette.

—J. R.

To Mom and Dad, with love and thanks.

—J. D.

Published by Raintree Publishers Inc.,
205 West Highland Avenue, Milwaukee, Wisconsin 53203.

Art Direction: Su Lund

Printed in the United States of America.

1 2 3 4 5 6 7 8 9 0 87 86 85 84 83

Library of Congress Cataloging in Publication Data
Reiser, Joanne.   Hannah's Alaska.   "A Carnival Press book."
Summary: Hannah helps her new friend adjust to life in Alaska, where moose, bears, and thirty-pound cabbages are common experiences. [1. Alaska—Fiction] I. Downing, Julie, ill. II. Title.
PZ7.R2774Han 1983   [E]   83-8668   ISBN 0-940742-23-3

One Saturday morning last winter our dog Oggie woke us with a loud bark.

"Somebody's here!" my sister shouted. Emily and I hurried to dress and see who it was.

"These are the Turners," my mother said. "They've just moved to Alaska and bought the cabin down the hill."

I couldn't believe the good news. Maybe at last I'd have a friend who lived nearby.

"I'm Zak," the boy told me, "and this is my sister Lila."

"My name is Hannah Lee Nichols," I said. Then I bit my tongue and wished I'd just said *Hannah.*

Pretty soon Emily was squealing and dragging Lila off to play with baby dolls.

"Come on, Zak," I said. "Let's go gather some eggs for breakfast."

"Hey, Hannah," Zak said, "if it's morning, where's the sun?"

"It's always this way in winter. There's just a little bit of light in the middle of the day."

"It isn't like that in California." Zak's voice sounded sad.

"Well, don't be homesick," I said quickly. "You'll get used to it here."

Inside the house Mrs. Turner stopped us. "Hannah, your mother says you walk to the bus stop in the dark—all by yourself!"

"*Do* you?" Zak's eyes opened wide.

"Well, yes, everybody does."

"I don't want to walk alone," Zak gulped. "Call me on Monday when you're ready to go."

"Zak," I said gently, "nobody in the wilderness has a telephone yet."

Monday morning I stopped for Zak on my way to school. He was so bundled up he could hardly walk.

"Do you know it's forty degrees below zero?" he complained.

"Don't worry about it, Zak. Hop on my sled."

"H-A-N-N-A-H! H-A-N-N-A-H!"

Zak scanned the trees with his flashlight. "Wh-Who's calling?" he asked.

"It's the kids down at the bus stop," I said. "They're not as close as they sound. When it's cold like this, you can hear things from far away."

"I bet you've never seen a bear," Nathan Morgan teased Zak at the bus stop.

"Don't be scared," I whispered to him. "Bears only come out in the spring."

At lunch I pointed out the windows. "See, Zak, this is the time of day we get a little light."

"But it will be dark again when we go home. I don't know if I like it here. My mother doesn't."

Somehow I would have to change his mind.

After school I told Zak about the northern lights.
"They're streamers of color that light up our sky
sometimes. Oggie barks when he hears them."

Zak stopped walking. "Are they loud, like firecrackers?"

"No, they sound like radio static. *Ppftt, sstfk*—like
that."

"You're fooling me," Zak sniffed.

"No, I'm not. Watch sometime and you'll see."

Even Mrs. Turner thought our northern lights were beautiful.

By the middle of March, daylight lasted longer—each day brought seven more minutes of sun.

Early in May we all drove to the Chena River to watch spring breakup. "Some people say they can feel it when the ice is ready to snap," I told Zak.

CRA-A-A-CK! BOOM! BOOM!

Chunks of ice flew up in the air and rivers of cold water gushed over the banks. We had to run for our trucks before the flood reached us.

The following Sunday, Zak and Lila came over to play.

"Look!" Zak shouted, pointing out the window.
"There's a bear by your chicken coop."

"We'll have to frighten it away," Father told us. "I loaned my gun to the Morgans."

CLANG CLANG! Zak and I beat pots and pans together
while Father took out his slingshot and beaned the bear.
"It's gone now," Father said, "but I'd better get my gun
back—just in case."

23

The sun came back, as we say in Alaska, and it was summer. There was no nighttime, no darkness.

Zak and I spent most of our time playing on the Chena River.

"This is the best place I ever lived," he told me.

"Does your mother like it here now?" I asked.

"Well, she hasn't talked so much about moving lately."

At harvest time Zak and I helped Mrs. Turner bring in the last vegetables from her garden.

"This cabbage must weigh over thirty pounds," Mrs. Turner said proudly.

Suddenly something crashed through the woods.
Before we could move, three moose—as big as trucks—
wandered into the clearing.

"Don't scream," I cautioned. "They just came here to
eat."

"Then give them the cabbage!" Zak whispered.

"No." I shook my head. "That would startle them, and
they might charge."

"Mommy, where are you?" Lila sang out from the house.

"Don't you dare come out here!" Mrs. Turner wailed. The huge bull laid back his ears and lowered his head.

"Walk back *quietly*," I said. We held on to each other and slowly backed up. The house seemed miles behind us.

"EE-EE-EE!" Lila screamed from the porch. That did it! We all turned and ran for the door.

When we looked out the window, we saw the moose munching on vegetable stalks.

"I guess moose won't hurt you," Mrs. Turner said slowly, "if you leave them alone."

"Hannah knew just what to do." Zak grinned at me.

Mrs. Turner smiled too. "If we can survive moose in our garden, we can survive *anything* in Alaska."

From the way she said it, I knew my friend Zak was here to stay.

Author **Joanne Reiser** has a writing and "sometimes acting" career that includes radio, television, newspapers, and national magazines. She and her husband Howard, a general surgeon, live in Joliet, Illinois, and have seven children.

The author says: "I first met Hannah when I wrote a newspaper feature about her family. They were visiting Illinois from Alaska. The more I questioned Hannah, the more I wanted to write this book!"

Artist **Julie Downing** was born in Denver, Colorado. After graduating from the Rhode Island School of Design with a major in illustration, she worked at the Smithsonian Institute and the Denver Museum of Natural History. Ms. Downing's love for young people is evident in the children's art classes she has taught in Denver at the Denver Children's Museum and in San Francisco, her current home. She has been a freelance illustrator in San Francisco for the past several years.